CH00847520

This Sunbear 🐻 Book belongs to:

_____

ISBN 981-04-9884-5

Published by:
SUNBEAR PUBLISHING PTE. LTD.

© SUNBEAR PUBLISHING PTE. LTD.

First published 2003
Second edition 2004
Third edition 2005
Reprint 2006

All rights reserved. No part of this publication may be reproduced
or transmitted in any form or by any means, electronic or mechanical,
including photocopying, or by any information storage and retrieval system,
without permission in writing from the Publisher.

Printed in Singapore

SASHA visits the ZOO

Illustrated by Alpana
Written by Shamini

Book Two: Sasha in Singapore

Sasha is at the Zoo.

A large bird struts past.

"Mamma! What's that?"

"It's a peacock, Sasha.

It has a long tail that opens like a fan."

Isn't it beautiful?!

A powerful, white polar bear swims right past Sasha.

He is looking for some fish for lunch.

He has huge paws!

Did you know the zoo keeps a part of
the polar bear enclosure air-conditioned?

Polar bears usually live where it is cold
and there is a lot of ice.

What are all the children looking at?

It is a family of meerkats.

The meerkats look worried!

Perhaps they can hear the lions roar....

There is a lion!

He looks big and fierce.

No wonder the meerkats look worried....

"Sasha, can you see the lion cub over there?"

"Can we take him home, Mamma?"

"No, darling. He would miss his Mamma!"

"Mamma, look! Look! I can see teddy!"

Sasha is right! The sun bears do look like her teddy.

The bears are called sun bears because
they have a patch of yellow on their chests.

Sun bears love to eat honey!

Hip, hip hooray!

Sasha and the orang utan wave their hands in the air!

Did you know that "orang utan" means
"man of the jungle"?

The orang utan does look like an old man, doesn't he?

Sasha is walking through the Fragile Forest.

There are birds, bats and butterflies!

She is looking at a black and white butterfly.

"What other animals can you see, Sasha?

Can you see a mousedeer and a lemur as well?"

"What do you have in your hands, Sasha?

Is it a ball of cotton wool?"

"It is a fluffy rabbit, Mamma!"

"Be gentle with it, Sasha!"

Sasha takes a ride on the zoo train.

There are other people on the train too....

Sasha can see a zebra and
two long-necked giraffes from the train.

Can you see them too?

Sasha is at home in bed after her exciting day at the zoo.

She is saying good night to her toy animals....

Can you spot the animals she saw at the zoo today?

Other Sunbear 🧸 Books
available in this series: